W9-DBF-074

Read-About® Geography

Georgia

By Carmen Bredeson

Consultant
Nanci Vargus, Ed. D.
Primary Multiage Teacher
Decatur Township Schools, Indianapolis, Indiana

Children's Press®
A Division of Scholastic Inc.
New York   Toronto   London   Auckland   Sydney
Mexico City   New Delhi   Hong Kong
Danbury, Connecticut

MAY 08

Designer: Herman Adler Design
Photo Researcher: Caroline Anderson
The photo on the cover shows part of the Okefenokee Swamp in Georgia.

Library of Congress Cataloging-in-Publication Data

Bredeson, Carmen.
  Georgia / by Carmen Bredeson.
      p. cm. — (Rookie read-about geography)
Includes index.
Summary: Introduces the state of Georgia, including its diverse geographical
features, agricultural crops, wildlife, cities, and famous citizens.
  ISBN 0-516-22670-3 (lib. bdg.)   0-516-27497-X (pbk.)
  1. Georgia—Juvenile literature. [1. Georgia.] I. Title. II. Series.
  F286.3 .B74 2002
  975.8—dc21

                                     2002005503

CHILDREN'S PRESS, AND ROOKIE READ-ABOUT®,
and associated logos are trademarks and or registered trademarks
of Grolier Publishing Co., Inc. SCHOLASTIC and associated logos
are trademarks and or registered trademarks of Scholastic Inc.

2 3 4 5 6 7 8 9 10 R 11 10 09 08 07 06 05

Do you know which state is called the Peach State?

The state of Georgia!
Georgia is located in the
southeast part of the
United States. Can you
find it on this map?

CANADA

WASHINGTON

OREGON

IDAHO

MONTANA

NORTH DAKOTA

SOUTH DAKOTA

WYOMING

NEVADA

UTAH

CALIFORNIA

COLORADO

ARIZONA

NEW MEXICO

MINNESOTA

MICHIGAN

WISCONSIN

IOWA

NEBRASKA

KANSAS

OKLAHOMA

TEXAS

ILLINOIS

INDIANA

MISSOURI

ARKANSAS

LOUISIANA

MISSISSIPPI

ALABAMA

NEW HAMPSHIRE

VERMONT

MAINE

NEW YORK

MASSACHUSETTS

RHODE ISLAND

CONNECTICUT

PENNSYLVANIA

NEW JERSEY

DELAWARE

OHIO

WEST VIRGINIA

MARYLAND

Washington, D.C.

VIRGINIA

KENTUCKY

TENNESSEE

NORTH CAROLINA

SOUTH CAROLINA

GEORGIA

FLORIDA

ALASKA

CANADA

MEXICO

HAWAII

North

West   East

South

5

There are mountains and waterfalls in the northern part of Georgia. The highest waterfall is called Amicalola.

The forests in Georgia have oak, poplar, and pine trees.

Brown thrashers build
nests in the tall trees.
The brown thrasher is
Georgia's state bird.

10

The weather in Georgia can be cold in the winter. Summer is always nice and warm. Plants grow well in the warm sunshine.

The land in Georgia
is good for farming.
Farmers grow cotton,
corn, peanuts, peaches,
and other important crops.

13

The Okefenokee Swamp is found in southern Georgia. The swamp is full of mud and rotting plants.

Alligators poke their noses
out of the brown water.
Wood storks build nests in
the trees.

Part of Georgia is next to the Atlantic Ocean. People like to visit the sandy beaches.

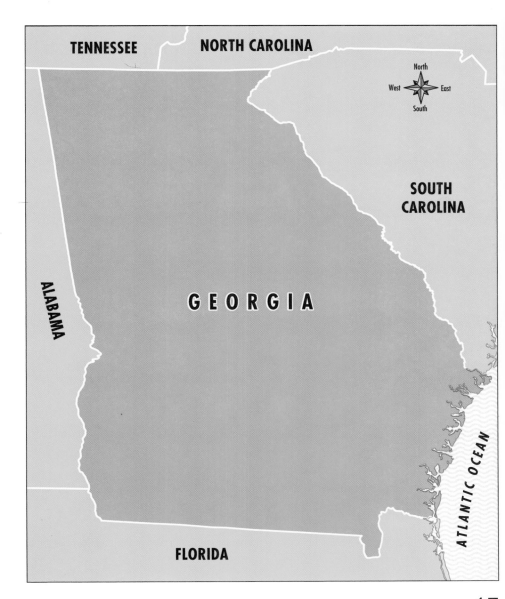

There are islands off the coast of Georgia. You can see wild horses, sea turtles, and many kinds of birds on these islands.

Fishermen from Georgia catch shrimp, crab, and fish in the ocean.

Atlanta is the capital of Georgia. Laws are made in the state capitol building.

Millions of people live in and around Atlanta. They work in tall office buildings, stores, and factories.

The main office for Coca-Cola is in Atlanta. You can visit the Coca-Cola museum.

Savannah is a smaller, quieter Georgia city. Beautiful houses line the streets. Shady parks give people a place to enjoy nature.

What is your favorite
place in Georgia?

Words You Know

Amicalola

Atlanta

beaches

brown thrasher

Okefenokee Swamp

peaches

Savannah

shrimp

Index

About the Author

Carmen Bredeson is the author of twenty-five books for children. She lives in Texas and enjoys doing research and traveling.

Photo Credits

Photographs © 2002: David R. Frazier: 13 top, 20, 31 bottom right; H. Armstrong Roberts, Inc.: 3, 31 top right (Camerique), 29 (Joe Maher), 25 (H. Sutton); Image Bank/J. Carmichael: 6, 30 top left; Peter Arnold Inc./Jeff Greenberg: 23; Photo Researchers, NY/M.P. Kahl: 15; Stone/Getty Images: 8 (James Randklev), 24, 30 top right, (Ron Sherman); Superstock, Inc.: 26, 31 bottom left; Tom Till: cover; Transparencies, Inc.: 16, 30 bottom left (Susan K. McElveen), 19 (Jim McGuire), 14, 31 top left (Chip Padgett); Unicorn Stock Photos: 10 (Dick Keen), 11 (Martha McBride), 9, 30 bottom right (Ted Rose); Visuals Unlimited/Inga Spence: 13 bottom.

Maps by Bob Italiano